To Glenn,

Thanks for teaching me to smell the snow.

Randy

BIG PIG AND THE LOST ELF

BY

RANDY BRILEY

BIG PIG WOKE WITH A SQUEAL
(BECAUSE CHRISTMAS WAS HERE),
DONNED HIS SCARF, CURLED HIS TAIL,
AND THEN WENT TO SPREAD CHEER.
TO THE FARM, HE LET OUT
A MOST MARVELOUS YELP.
THIS YEAR'S GIFT? NOT MUD PIES...
INSTEAD, HE'D GIVE HELP.

THE HENS BALKED AT HIS OFFER. THEY JUST DIDN'T LIKE GAMBLIN'
ON THE EGGS THAT THEY KNEW THAT THE PIG WOULD BE SCRAMBLIN'.

NEXT, THE PIG WENT TO TRIM ALL THE WOOL OFF THE SHEEP.
THEY SAID "BAA" WHEN ALL DONE AND THEY WANTED TO WEEP.

HE DECIDED TO PLOW BUT IT DID NOT MAKE SENSE.
WHY DON'T TRACTORS HAVE BRAKES? WHY NO GATES IN THE FENCE?

ON AND ON THROUGH THE DAY, 'TIL THE FARM WAS OFFENDED.
"GO AWAY," THEY ALL CRIED AND HIS CHRISTMAS JOY ENDED.

THEN CAME A LOUD SCREAM THAT DID NOT SEEM TO STOP.

FROM ABOVE A LOUD, "AHHHHHHHH!" THEN NEARBY, A "KERPLOP"!

IN THE SNOW SAT AN ELF, LOOKING SPUN, FLIPPED, AND TOSSED, WEARING CLOTHES THAT WERE RUMPLED. PIG KNEW IT WAS LOST.

"I'LL HELP YOU!" SAID THE PIG, BOUNCING OUT OF CONTROL.
"I'LL FIND THIS STRANGE PLACE THAT YOU CALL THE "NORTH POLE!"

SINCE THE PIG HAD NOT TRAVELED, THEY MADE SOME MISTAKES,
BUT THE ELF DIDN'T MIND: HE JUST SHARED HIS FRUITCAKES.

"SHOULD THE NORTH POLE BE HOT?" ASKED THE PIG, QUITE DISMAYED.
"NO, NEVER," SQUEAKED THE ELF AS HE SCRAMBLED FOR SHADE.

"SHOULD IT BE SO HIGH UP?" PIG SAID, GETTING SADDER.
"N-NO," SAID THE ELF, YELLING UP FROM THE LADDER.

THEY WENT THAT WAY AND THIS WAY AND OFTEN WERE WRONG
BUT THEY FILLED UP THEIR TIME WITH A JOKE OR A SONG.

SOME PLACES WERE SCARY. "YEOWWWW!" THEY WOULD YELL
(THOSE DEADLY PIRANHAS COULD SWIM REALLY WELL).

"BONG, BONG, BONG!"

OTHER PLACES WERE GREY AND THE RAIN WAS QUITE STRONG
BUT EVERY NEW PLACE HAD ITS OWN SPECIAL SONG.

SOME PLACES WERE THRILLING WITH SO MUCH TO SEE.
THEY COULDN'T RIDE BIKES WITHOUT SHOUTING, "WEEEEE!"

IF THEY FOUND THEMSELVES LOST, WITH HEADS STARTING TO DROOP,
THEY WOULD ASK FOR DIRECTIONS: "ZOOBITY, BOP, BOOP?"

THROUGH IT ALL, PIG HAD ELF, AND ELF ALWAYS HAD PIG
SO IT JUST DIDN'T MATTER IF THINGS GOT TOO BIG.

ON DAYS THE ELF LED, "THIS WAY, PIG!" HE LIKED SHOUTIN'
IN THE DAY AND AT NIGHT, FROM THE SEA TO THE MOUNTAIN.

FOR THE REST OF THE TIME IT WAS BIG PIG WHO LED.
"THERE'S A SOUTH POLE? YOU'RE KIDDING? IS THAT WHAT THEY SAID?"

THROUGH TWISTS, LOOPS, AND TURNS, SOMETIMES UP AND THEN DOWN,
THE TWO STUCK TOGETHER THROUGH TOWN AFTER TOWN.

THEY BOTH GREW TO LIKE IT, JUST TO WANDER AND ROAM

BUT WERE ALSO QUITE HAPPY WHEN THEY FOUND THE ELF'S HOME.

"HIP, HOORAY!" THE ELVES CHEERED AND THEY GAVE THEM BOTH HUGS.
ALL THEIR SPIRITS WERE HIGH WITH NO SCROOGE-Y "HUMBUGS".

THEN SANTA TOLD BIG PIG, "YOU HAVE SUCH A KIND SOUL!
WE'LL MAKE YOU AN 'ELF', FRIEND TO ALL THE NORTH POLE!"

BIG PIG SMILED AND LAUGHED AND THEY ALL HAD A BLAST!
AND HIS LITTLE ELF FRIEND SAVED THE BEST HUG FOR LAST.

ON THE RIDE HOME THAT NIGHT, AS THE ELF HELD THE PIG,
THEY BOTH MADE A WISH WITH THEIR HEARTS FEELING BIG:

THAT NO MATTER THE PLACE AND NO MATTER THE WEATHER
THEY WOULD FIND THE BEST WAY TO SPEND CHRISTMAS TOGETHER.

ONCE BACK ON THE FARM (JUST 'TIL CHRISTMAS NEXT YEAR)
BIG PIG OPENED HIS GIFTS, SMILING EAR TO PINK EAR.

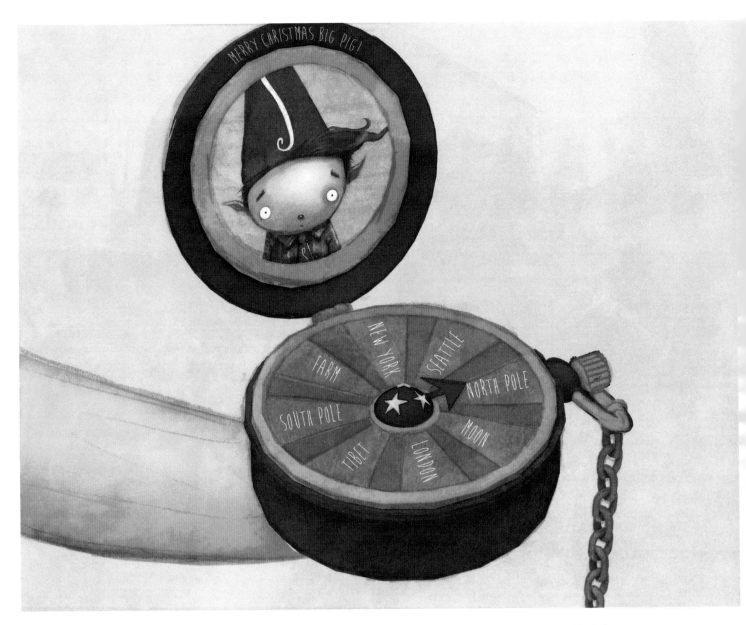

'TWAS A SHINY NEW COMPASS HE COULD USE AS A GUIDE
FROM THE BEST FRIEND OF ALL, WHO WOULD WALK BY HIS SIDE.

MERRY CHRISTMAS!

For more information about this book and other exciting projects from artist and author Randy Briley, please visit:

ravenmadstudios.com

37601275R00024

Made in the USA
Lexington, KY
08 December 2014